Take a Kiss to School

For Ginny – A.M.

With special thanks to the Reception Class of 2003/04
at Oakthorpe School, Enfield – S.H.

Text copyright © 2006 by Angela McAllister
Illustrations copyright © 2006 by Sue Hellard

Typeset in Garamond Infant
Art created with ink and watercolor
Design by Sarah Hodder

Published by Bloomsbury Publishing, New York, London, and Berlin
Distributed to the trade by Holtzbrinck Publishers

Library of Congress Cataloging-in-Publication Data
McAllister, Angela.
Take a kiss to school / by Angela McAllister ; illustrated by Sue Hellard.—1st U.S. ed.
p. cm.
Summary: Digby's mother helps him make it through the second day of school by
sending him off with a pocket full of kisses.
ISBN-10: 1-58234-702-6 • ISBN-13: 978-1-58234-702-8
[1. Schools—Fiction. 2. Moles (Animals)—Fiction. 3. Animals—Fiction.]
I. Hellard, Susan, ill. II. Title.
PZ7.M47825Tak 2006   [E]—dc22   2005053689

First U.S. Edition 2006
Printed in China
1 3 5 7 9 10 8 6 4 2

Bloomsbury Publishing, Children's Books, U.S.A.
175 Fifth Avenue, New York, NY 10010

All papers used by Bloomsbury Publishing are natural, recyclable products
made from wood grown in well-managed forests. The manufacturing processes
conform to the environmental regulations of the country of origin.

Take a Kiss to School

by Angela McAllister
illustrated by Sue Hellard

BLOOMSBURY
CHILDREN'S
BOOKS

The first day Digby went to school, he learned how to line up in the playground, where to hang his jacket, and how to say, "Yes, Mrs. Hoot," when the teacher called his name. He played with sand, sang rhymes, and painted a picture for his mother.

oakthorpe School

"Did you have a good time?" asked his father.
"Yes," said Digby.

The next morning, his mother opened the curtains.

"Time to get up for school."

"No," said Digby. "I went there yesterday."

"You have to go again," she explained. "You're a schoolboy now."

"No, I'm not," said Digby. "I want to stay here with you." And he hid under the covers.

But Digby had to go to school.

"Why are you worried?" asked his mother as they walked to school through the woods.

"I've forgotten where to line up and where to hang my jacket," said Digby. "I might not hear the teacher when she calls my name."

"I'll be there to put you in line," said his mother.

Digby wrinkled his nose unhappily. "I want you to stay all day."

"No," she said. "I can't do that."

When they got to school, Digby stopped at the gate.

"I'm not going in without you."

His mother gave him a hug. Then she had an idea.
She cupped her hands, blew a dozen kisses, and slipped
them into Digby's pocket.

"There! If you're worried, you can take a kiss
from your pocket and imagine I am with you."
Digby squeezed her tight.
"Oops . . . don't squash them!" she said.

The school bell rang, and all the children lined up
to go inside. Digby kept his jacket on.

When Mrs. Hoot called
his name, he answered
loud and clear.

But when it was time
to choose partners
for a clapping game,
Digby didn't know
what to do.

He dipped a hand into his pocket and then pressed it to his
cheek. It felt warm, just like a kiss from his mother. Digby smiled.
  "Will you be my partner?" asked a little girl named Otterly.
  "Yes," said Digby, and they clapped together.

At playtime, Digby sat on the
bench. All the other children ran
around together. Nobody asked
him to join in.

Then Digby took a kiss from his pocket
and pressed it to his cheek. He felt
a little bit braver.
Digby stood up
and took a
step forward.

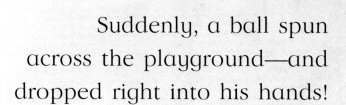

Suddenly, a ball spun
across the playground—and
dropped right into his hands!

"Throw it back," called
the other children.
"Come and play!"

After playtime, Mrs. Hoot
read a story. Then the
class talked about it.
Digby even raised
his hand to answer
a question.

line here

We all eat

different food.

Have you found your bag?

walk, don't run!

But at lunchtime there were lots of things to remember.

"Boys and girls with lunch boxes go to that table. Children having school lunch line up here. Get your drinks from the tray on the cart. Don't start eating until everyone is sitting down," said Mrs. Hoot.

Digby felt worried again. If only his mother were there to tell him what to do. Once more he took a kiss from his pocket and held it tightly.

"Digby," said Mrs. Hoot, "you can sit here beside me."
And she showed him just what to do.

After lunch, the class had playtime again. Everyone
took off their jackets in the warm sun—even Digby.
One of the boys gave him the ball, and soon he
was having great fun.

In the afternoon, Mrs. Hoot asked the children to stand
up one at a time and tell the class about their families.
Digby didn't want to stand up in front of everyone.
He felt like he needed one of his mother's
kisses—but he'd left his jacket outside!
Digby ran to the playground to find it.

Digby found his jacket on the playground.
But when he put it on, he saw the pocket
was ripped! He put his finger through the
hole. The pocket felt cold and empty.

"The kisses have fallen out!" Digby
gasped. His nose began to quiver.
Just then, he heard someone crying.
It was Otterly.

"What's the matter?" asked Digby.

"I can't find the water
fountain," said Otterly,
"and I don't want to ask."
"I know where it is,"
said Digby. "I saw it at
lunchtime."

Digby took Otterly to the water fountain. Then they went back to class together.

"Can I sit next to you, Digby?" whispered Otterly.

"Yes," said Digby.

For the rest of the day,
Otterly sat beside Digby.
He sharpened her pencil,

found her an apron,

and explained things
she didn't understand.

Digby forgot about the pocketful of kisses until it was time
to go home.

His mother was waiting at the gate. She gave Digby a hug.

"Can I go back tomorrow?" he asked. "I made a new friend."

"Did you need your pocketful of kisses?" asked his mother.

Digby showed her the empty pocket.

"They fell out," he said with a frown.

Just then, Otterly appeared wearing exactly the same jacket as Digby!

"You've got mine," she said, laughing. "I caught the pocket on my bicycle coming to school."

Digby and Otterly swapped jackets.

"See you tomorrow," said Otterly.

"See you tomorrow," said Digby.

After dinner, Digby hung his bag on the end
of his bed.

"I don't think I'll need to take kisses to
school tomorrow," he decided with a yawn.

"Oh, good," said his mother, tucking him in.
"But I hope schoolboys aren't too grown up
for good-night kisses?"

"Not me," said Digby happily. "Never!"